Penguin Specials fill a gap. Written by some of today's most exciting and insightful writers, they are short enough to be read in a single sitting – when you're stuck on a train; in your lunch hour; between dinner and bedtime. Specials can provide a thought-provoking opinion, a primer to bring you up to date, or a striking piece of fiction. They are concise, original and affordable.

To browse digital and print Penguin Specials titles, please refer to **penguin.com.au/penguinspecials**

ALSO BY ANNA FUNDER

Stasiland
All That I Am

The Girl with the Dogs

ANNA FUNDER

PENGUIN BOOKS

UK | USA | Canada | Ireland | Australia
India | New Zealand | South Africa | China

Penguin Books is part of the Penguin Random House group of companies
whose addresses can be found at global.penguinrandomhouse.com.

Penguin
Random House
Australia

First published as *Everything Precious* by Paspaley Group, 2014
This edition published by Penguin Group (Australia), 2015

Copyright © Anna Funder 2014

The moral right of the author has been asserted

Cover illustration by Grace West © Penguin Group (Australia)
Printed and bound in Australia by Griffin Press,
an accredited ISO AS/NZS 14001 Environmental Management Systems printer.

National Library of Australia Cataloguing-in-Publication data is available.

ISBN: 9780143573500

penguin.com.au

MIX
Paper | Supporting
responsible forestry
FSC® C018684

For Jo Ann Hopkins and Peter Bracher

I

It is late and the day – like most of them now – has been both long and not nearly long enough to get everything done. From their bedroom Tess and Dan can hear Charlotte, their eldest, still talking on her phone so they keep their voices down. Sound travels in this house – a skinny terrace in a reasonably fashionable area, though for the price of it they could have moved out to the suburbs and had a pool and ensuites with his-and-hers sinks like the children wanted.

Dan is propped up on the pillows with his iPad.

You could never know, Tess thinks, what he is reading or buying or who he's talking to on that thing. At least in the olden days you could distinguish between a book and a shop and a telephone. Tess works in legal publishing but on the editing, rather than the online side of it. She steps out of her skirt.

'Weird thing happened today,' Dan says without taking his eyes off the screen. 'I got Facebooked by Sukie.'

'Sukie . . .?' she says, taking a hanger from the wardrobe. Though she knows full well. How many Sukies does anyone know?

'Yep. Weird. She said, "Seems like everything's going great in your life. So glad for you."' He looks up at his wife and shudders in an exaggerated way. 'I haven't heard from her in . . .' he glances at the ceiling, 'must be eighteen years.'

Tess and Dan have been together seventeen years.

She finds her pyjamas where she left them, screwed up under the pillow. Sukie was Dan's first long-term girlfriend. She turned out to be Completely Not Right, though how 'completely' could that be if it took him four years to figure it out? Like most couples Tess knows, she and Dan don't talk about each other's sexual history before they got together. Except after a couple of drinks, when Tess has been known to refer to Dan's life

2

before her as having involved mistakes, apprentice-ships and witches. Dan is more loyal to his past, in a way she both respects and wishes he would abandon. She would like him, just once, to rain vitriol on his exes, but then again that would take away from the very tolerance and fairness she loves him for, blah, blah.

'Did you message her back?'

'Yes.' He leans over on one elbow towards her and the light catches the creases at the corners of his eyes. 'I told her about my lovely life, and my lovely, lovely wife.'

It is impossible to know, at this stage in a marriage, and with this kind of smile, whether his tone covers something sincere and tender, or not.

'You didn't say that,' she says.

'No, that would have been mean. I just said we're fine thanks, and told her about the children.'

She looks past his stubbly chin and sees he's been reading an online medical journal. Once, bringing him coffee in the study, she'd read an email over his shoulder. It praised a postdoctoral student's 'warmth and deep sensitivity' and offered to meet her for dinner on the first night of the conference in Puerto Rico. This is what infidelity looks like, she'd thought: the banality of it in black and white, the cursor pulsing expectantly. There were certain paths she did not wish to think her way down. Whatever the sustaining illusions of her marriage were, they would, like the fragile planks of a bridge over a deepening chasm, not survive her hurtling across them. When she'd asked him what he thought he was doing, he said, 'Nothing.' And then he said, 'Trying to be encouraging.' Tess had consigned the episode to a black hole of history out of which she was the winner, simply because she was here in the present tense, and the student – so far as she knew – was not.

She hesitates, half in her pyjamas, watching him read.

He looks up and smiles again and in that instant he is a man with no past, who wishes only to love his wife, standing there in front of him. He is a man whose purity of current intent obliterates – as it should in moments when thought is not called for – anything else.

She pulls the covers back to get in. 'If you wanted to stalk someone you used to have to act crazy *in reality*, and park your car outside their house,' she says. 'Now it's just click click click and you're indistinguishable from all the other crazies on the internet.'

'You're the crazy woman,' Dan says, placing the iPad on the nightstand and turning round to her. And possibly it is true.

II

Breakfast.

The twins are six, Tom and Lorna. Charlotte is thirteen. There has been plenty of time – years and years – to institute routines of breakfast-and-lunch-making but still every day is different and unpredictable, despite having half the lunches prepared the night before (not the sandwiches, or the kids won't eat them for sogginess). Tess has no idea when it began – probably at weaning – but each child has exactly what they want, every single item, for breakfast and for lunch. In her more capable moments this seems like modern, considerate family life. At other, rattier times it feels like indulgent insanity, the revenge-parenting her generation is quietly, effortfully taking on its baby-boomer parents, those distracted giants who'd grunted over their newspapers at the cereal cupboard and felt their job was done. She finishes wiping yoghurt out of her hair with a damp tea towel (Tom had been making a point with his spoon) and turns back to the chopping board.

'Is it Fuji?' Lorna's little legs are swinging from the kitchen barstool. Lorna will only eat Fuji apples. '*Is it Fuji?*' Lorna has interrogated the crescents on her plate since she was three. Tess always says yes, no matter what kind of apple it is. This is exactly the kind of mothering dishonesty she wants to avoid, but there it is already.

Her own mother had sometimes, but not always, put raw egg into breakfast milkshakes for Tess and her brother, so as to make sure they got some 'real protein' in the days when they binned their soggy sandwiches and lived on Twisties from the tuckshop. It was impossible to taste the egg, but the idea of it made Tess gag. Her mother would laugh and compare herself to the French government, 'neither confirming nor denying' the presence of nuclear warheads on their ships in the Pacific (it was the '80s). The whole period was unappetising.

She hears the rise and fall of voices upstairs: Charlotte and her father having the usual argument about whatever boundary Charlotte is pushing today. Lately it has been about texting till midnight and Instagramming endless selfies to friends, as if to reassure everyone, including herself, of her continuing existence outside of school hours. Charlotte pleads that if they take her phone away she turns up at school the next day and 'has missed everything'. Tess and Dan both want her to have some relief from the demands of curating her virtual double. But for Tess it's more than that – she does not want her daughter to be the only one who is left out due to retrograde parental practices. Tess hadn't been allowed to watch television on weeknights ('It'll rot your mind,' her mother said). Almost as much as she wants to protect Charlotte, she doesn't want to be that awful mother.

Tom has picked the raisins out of a bowl of milky cereal and is threading them onto a fork. His cowlick makes a wodge of hair stick straight up off his forehead.

'Is metal stronger than steel or steel stronger than metal?' He lisps a little, having recently lost his two top front teeth.

She takes the fork out of his hand and substitutes

a spoon, giving her time to think.

'Steel is a kind of metal,' she says.

'Is grey hair older than white hair or white hair older than grey hair?'

She draws breath. Every day there are questions that are tests. She tries to answer them both truthfully and without making reality too shocking. ('We eat baby lambs? And the pigs – do we eat their babies too?') She knows these questions are not about animals, but about them: *What kind of monsters are we?* But sometimes comfort and truth are not compatible, or the truth is complicated in ways that lose the attention of a six-year-old. Her father Howard had been a judge, and his father a surgeon. For every difficult question of her childhood, for instance about sex or cancer, her father had answered legally accurately (preferably with Latin) and using obscure medical terms ('lesion' for tumour, 'procedure' for operation). So although he could never be accused of lying he could also never, quite, be understood.

The thought occurs to her: Perhaps her father aimed to spare her – as well as himself – the trauma of the world? She wishes she could ask him, but that question would be too complicated for him now.

Lorna is ignoring her breakfast altogether, sifting instead through the eternal tide of detritus that washes up on the end of the bench – currently including homeless puzzle pieces, subscription renewal forms, propelling pencils with no leads, and a green rubber ball designed to be spat out by a one-eyed foam monster no one has seen for weeks. Lorna finds a pair of huge black 3D-movie glasses and puts them on.

'Mu-um?' Tom bleats.

'Sorry.' Tess sips her coffee. 'Well. Sometimes quite young people get grey or white hair. And sometimes old people don't go either grey or white. But you're right: grey and white are both old people's hair colours.'

Tom's face gives nothing away.

She hears a miniature version of Dr Preston, her therapist, on her right shoulder: 'Watch those thought patterns, Tess; can you see them becoming grim and circular? Try to be fully *present* with your children.' But on her left shoulder squats the Evil Imp of Anxiety, snubbing its snub little nose at Dr P and continuing its endless, wicked work of list-making. Today, she's 'working at home' and hers is:

- meet real estate agent (poor Lizzie)
- visit Dad
- finish conference paper (wobbly middle section)

- possible leg/chin/bikini wax
- postpone Charlotte's parent–teacher interview
- pack
- find passport

She is leaving for the London conference ('Innovative Legal Publishing in the Digital Age') tomorrow. Twenty-two hours in a plane with 399 other people – a plight which seems, from this moment in the kitchen, a barely conceivable luxury of solitude.

A pair of familiar – though also strange – legs in ankle socks and school shoes starts down the stairs. Charlotte's uniform is hoiked up to reveal most of her thighs, which are unnaturally dark and mottled from fake tan, and she has painted eyeliner on flamboyantly, like an Italian film star from the 1960s, or a dead soul-punk chanteuse. But instead of Amy Winehouse it's the words 'Agent Orange' that spring to mind when Tess looks at her daughter. Dan follows, deliberately unhurried.

'Not sure they let raccoons into school,' he says to the room at large. Dan is head of epidemiology in the state health department. He has a knack, honed in endless intra-agency meetings, for opening out a conflict from the parties involved so it becomes a matter for all to discuss. Charlotte rolls her eyes in their kohl-rimmed sockets and starts stuffing books into her backpack.

'Though they might think you're a new exchange student,' Dan smiles. There had been some Pacific Islander girls at school last term.

'That's racist,' Charlotte snaps.

'I'm kidding,' he says.

'Still racist.'

'I think you're pretty,' Lorna says, turning her face, behind the oversized frames, towards her sister. For her, Charlotte is a goddess – one who can turn mean at any second, but then that is the way of goddesses. Charlotte swivels away.

Tess leans across to Lorna. 'Are they magic glasses, then?'

Dan shoots her a look. He moves to Charlotte.

'You're beautiful,' he says, daring to touch her shoulder. 'Especially without all that,' he gestures to her, top to toe.

'You must be blind!' Charlotte cries. Tears spring up in her eyes.

Why a compliment or sympathy should make us cry Tess has never understood, but it does. Every woman she knows has a secret list of faults she keeps in her heart, unnecessary and malign. How did it get there? She wants, more than anything, to save her daughters from this.

Charlotte goes into the bathroom and slams the door. She will emerge in a few minutes with smudged eyes and the eyeliner pencil concealed in her pocket.

Tess closes Tom and Lorna's backpacks, and gets to the final thing: sunscreen. Tom tilts his face to her, closing his eyes tight. His mouth makes a scrunched-up star, ready for the smear.

'When are you going to die, Mum?' He is matter-of-fact because death doesn't apply to him, and in any case it's not necessarily all that debilitating. Things in his world – Power Rangers, Ninjagos, Red Riding Hood from inside the wolf's stomach – come back to life all the time.

'But I don't have any grey hair or white hair.'

'But when?' he insists.

'Not for a very long time,' she says, as casually as possible, smoothing cream over his tiny nostrils. She looks about for something wooden, spies the handle of the breadknife and taps it quickly. Then places her fingers back under his chin. Tom opens his eyes, which are blue and intricately faceted as marbles.

'Before me or after me?'

Tess knows this little soul. He doesn't want to be left alone – not in the dark, not on the first day at school, and not in the end. Who does? There's no

Latin, no legalese for this.

She takes a deep breath.

'Before you,' she says, hoping this is true, and also, as she holds his perfect, shiny face, not true at all. 'You'll be an old man with a family of your own to look after you,' she adds, 'and I'll be a very old lady, all done.'

All done? What on earth —? That is taking list-thinking way, way too far. She will never, ever be all done here.

III

After dropping the little ones at school, she drives across town. A month ago they moved her father into Hopetown Village Senior Living Facility and now the house she grew up in is for sale. A billboard stands out the front. It says: 'Grand Family Home or Development Opportunity STCA'. It also says: 'Harbour Glimpses', which Tess feels bad about because she knows they are only from the bottom corner of the left side dormer window in the attic. The board has photographs of the rooms in the house taken with a fisheye lens, which makes them look swollen, and a larger one of the whole house at dusk with all the lights on, looming like a ship adrift on the lawn. It is the kind of house no one she knows of her generation can afford.

She is meeting the real estate agent here – her friend Lizzie, just starting out in her own business. Tess has come early because she feels the house will cease to be hers not when a contract is signed, but when the first strangers step foot in it today.

The gate squeaks. The house is set back from the street, part hidden behind an old magnolia. A wide verandah wraps around it on three sides, festooned with wrought-iron lace. She walks up the path between the two palm trees, which meet the earth with their gigantic elephant's feet; she knows their scales intimately, as footholds.

Her phone beeps. A text message from Lizzie: *5 mins xx*. She wouldn't be Lizzie if she wasn't at least five minutes late.

Tess walks through the rooms, each one of them opening with double doors onto the verandah, or with windows onto the garden. Without their furniture, they have shrunk into themselves a little. The house used to be alive with the smells of cooking and cat fur and wood polish, strains of her father's beloved Mozart over the hum of the dryer and a timpani of copper-bottomed kitchen pans hanging from a rail. Her mother's Persian carpets are all gone; Tess's steps sound hollow on the floorboards. But she also hears children's voices, her brother's and her own. She slides the glass door from the kitchen to the back garden, and glimpses in its light-bending moment all of them – Dad, Mum, James and herself – having lunch at the table under the tulip tree. She is fourteen and that is her childhood, and now it is being sold.

The table is gone, but the stone bench is still under the tree. Tess sits. In the clear morning light the saltwater pool is the softest green. She stares at the gently ruffling surface. Pools have always made her happy, particularly this one. Then the breeze stops and she notices something at the bottom. It is a single, improbably intact porcelain cup. Without being able to read them, she knows the words on its side read: 'NSW Bar Association', under a blindfolded figure holding a scale.

Tess's father had been a good judge – very fair, and never stepping too far beyond the bounds of precedent so as to make sure he was rarely appealed. Outside of work, though, he'd left all decisions to his wife, as if he were sapped of making up his mind in chambers, and also as if the running of a life and a house, and the children and their lives, were somehow unreal to him, possibly even trivial, like the fleeting emotions of dogs.

After her mother died – though her father had never credited her with this power – it was as if he'd lost an engine. Not a large man, he dropped nine kilos. He left his wife's greeting on the answering machine for a year and a half. James said it was so they had to continue to reach their father, as ever, through their mother, but Tess wondered if it was a simple comfort, and if Howard called home ten times a day to hear it.

He sputtered forward gamely for some years till retirement. Last year he'd started to go for evening walks to clear his head, but then the streets tangled and looked unfamiliar and 'louts' had defaced the street signs, either by graffiti or popguns. Twice he'd had to be brought home by police.

Her phone beeps again but she doesn't move to get it from her bag. It'll be Lizzie, telling her she'll be another five minutes. Then Tess remembers that she has children and should look to see if one of them has forgotten something or has been abducted and is calling from the back of a van driven by dim, tattooed cretins.

Why does the motherly imagination curdle so quickly to horror? Dr Preston said it was evolution (to foresee and prevent dangers), but it feels more like a curse. Dan has tried to help things by putting a family-tracking app called Life360 on their phones. The kids' are kept in their backpacks (they aren't allowed to take them out at school), so hopefully – her grim, motherly imagination continues – as long as their backpacks are abducted with them, everything will be just fine.

She takes out her phone. 'Your monsters need feeding and changing!' It's a game the twins play. She taps it away.

Footsteps click down the side path.

'Hi-hi!' Lizzie puffs towards her in a snug skirt and heels, a small studded handbag over her shoulder. Tess stares. Lizzie has dyed her fairish hair deep red and had it cut in a sharp, fringed bob. It sits perfectly of a piece, like a helmet, on her head.

'Wow,' Tess says.

'I know. I'm in character.' Lizzie smiles cheesily and does a wobbly curtsey, brandishing a clipboard in one hand and a stack of glossy leaflets in the other.

'You look like a Lego piece.'

Lizzie laughs. 'From the movie? Agent Red?' She pats the bottom of her bob with a palm. 'Or just cheap and plasticky?'

Tess smiles. She is unsure whether her friend has what it takes for this line of work, which would be a mixture of cheery confidence and steely overkill.

Then she notices that Lizzie's nails are red, as are the patent tips of her shoes.

Lizzie and Tess performed in many student plays together, but only Lizzie had been brave enough to risk becoming a professional actress. Tess had been more practical, and got an editing qualification. After a long run in a popular TV drama Lizzie had the children and her career fizzled out. Though Tess is bored to the bone by her own working life, she sometimes catches herself thinking of Lizzie's fate as a vindication of her safer choice. Thinking this way digusts her, but it is not in her control. Lizzie has been working as a real estate agent since Terry left and became Terence, and that is a long story.

In fact, Tess and Dan's friendship group is ridden by midlife crises of varying degrees of spectacularity and cliché, often starting with the acquisition of what she thinks of as getaway vehicles – a Vespa, or a vintage Mercedes – which a husband suddenly realises he's been denying himself. Terry had been a kindly, elegant marketing executive for New South Wales Tourism. He came out as Terence in flannel shirts and driving a white ute. Dan was unfazed. He put his arm around his friend and said, 'All you need is a cattle dog,' but it turned out what Terence really needed was a nice construction lawyer called Mick Nguyen. Another friend, a long-time and parliamentary researcher who wore Blundstone boots and drank Tooheys, hadn't changed his sexuality or politics as far as they (yet) knew, but he had left his wife and taken to wearing cravats, drinking Pimm's, and carrying, on weekends, a silent, beady-eyed chihuahua named Coco in the pocket of his suit jacket. There were, of course, standard-issue affairs, where people seemed so relieved to feel once more the overwhelming love they'd felt when young for their spouse, that this feeling in itself made them feel young again – only with someone else's spouse. They traded a life of predictable comfort and trajectory for a more complicated one of child swaps and step-relationships, and felt, if more exhausted, at least (they told themselves) more alive.

And then there were those left over, like remainders in a sum.

'It must be hard, my love.' Lizzie sits, pulling her skirt down over her thighs like a tube. 'So many memories.'

Tess feels that whatever she is going through, it's nothing compared to what Lizzie has suffered. She admires her friend's practical courage, her daily, one-foot-in-front-of-the-other, chin-up managing. Lizzie has always thought of herself as someone smiled upon by invisible fates and is now, Tess sees, struggling valiantly to maintain this view. Lizzie frequently wins small amounts on scratch tickets, or is offered freebies from phone marketers (a car service, the chance of an island holiday). At restaurants when her dinner comes cold or underdone she sends it back with a big smile and is never billed. Lately, Lizzie has started to talk about herself as a character. She'll say, 'I'm the kind of person who's always forward-oriented,' and 'I've just got to get out of my own way,' as if saying it will make it so. Lizzie breaks Tess's heart. At the same time, though Tess knows that marital disaster is not contagious, part of her would prefer to pass it on by, eyes respectfully averted, as from a three-car pile-up.

'Oops – I forgot to put out the Open House sign.' Lizzie stands. Her phone beeps. She sits down again. 'Sorry. Could be work.' She looks at its screen. 'Terence and Mick are at Ha Long Bay,' she says. 'Nice for some!'

'He sends you messages?' Tess is trying to avoid what Charlotte calls 'tone' in her voice.

'No.' Lizzie blinks slowly. 'I follow him on Facebook. I get alerts when he posts something.'

'You're torturing yourself.'

Lizzie shrugs, not looking at her. 'I just like to know where he is,' she says.

Tess puts her arm around her friend. There's gone, she thinks, and then there's the afterlife bleeping in your bag. She can't think of anything except something silly to say. 'Can't live with 'em, can't live without 'em.'

Lizzie is making a dint in the gravel with the red point of her shoe. '*You've* got nothing to worry about,' she says. 'Dan is solid as a rock.'

People say this kind of thing out of the habits of friendship: both Tess and Lizzie know they can't be sure how 'solid' anyone is these days, including themselves. Tess chews the inside of her cheek.

They are at a hinge moment: between youth and age, between the life you thought you wanted and the one you feel might, now, suit you better. They are like hermit crabs who outgrow one shell and need to leave it before they are trapped inside, emerging for a moment, shell-less and pink, vulnerable to predators of every stripe.

'Hello? Is this the open house?' A woman's voice calls from the side fence.

'Give me five minutes?' Tess whispers, releasing her friend. 'I'll leave through the back gate.'

Lizzie makes a sympathetic face and squeezes Tess's hand. Then she rushes inside, sliding the glass door closed behind her.

The pool net has been tidied away along with

everything else. Quickly, Tess takes off her shoes, her watch and her jeans. Then she steps in, down and under, and souvenirs the cup.

IV

Tess drives home again to change – dripping wet but elated as a thief.

She gets to her father's room later than expected. Howard is sitting on a cushion on the floor in front of the television, which is turned up loud. On the screen a svelte young woman with close-cropped hair, apparently naked, straddles a concrete wrecking ball, holding onto its chain and singing fit to bust as she swings in, and then out, of frame. Her father moves his head to follow the girl swinging in, and then out again. The image is startling and

Howard looks startled. But also transfixed.

'Hi Dad.'

He turns his face up to her and smiles. 'Darling.' He shakes his head. 'I don't know about all this.' He throws the TV a guilty look.

'Me neither,' Tess says. 'Let's get you up.' She holds out her hands and he clasps them, but stays put.

'Reminds me of your mother,' he says in a small, cracked voice.

Is it the young woman's near-bald head that recalls her mother at the end? Or is he feeling some kind of lust that takes him back to her? Tess doesn't want to leave him bewildered and alone in his disinhibition, but then again, there are probably places it is just not right for a daughter to go. And, as she looks at his soft, lined face, he doesn't seem unhappy.

'Hi there.' The carer hesitates politely at the door. She is a cheery, solid young woman whose name Tess has forgotten. She has dreadlocks held back in a thick ponytail, several earrings in the cartilage of her left ear, and a tattoo of a woman riding a horse down one forearm. What these are signs of Tess does not know, for they are not signs intended for her.

'He loves his MTV.' The woman moves to help her father up. 'We watch it a lot, don't we,

Howard?' she says to him kindly. 'Loves his iPad, too. Found him curled up in bed with it a couple of times.'

'Thank you,' Tess quickly reads her name tag, 'Ella.' Then she remembers she's left a bag of things for her father – butterscotch, Depends, some CDs – in the car.

When she comes back Ella is in a chair pulled up close to her father's, singing to music coming from the iPad on his knee. Her voice is confident – perhaps she's a musician, just jobbing here? Tess walks around behind them.

Between the dreadlocks on one side and the white wisps of her father's hair on the other, she watches another young woman on the screen. This one is sitting in a chair with her head thrown back, singing. Between her parted legs a man kneels, inching a white garter down her thigh with his teeth. Then the woman, insanely beautiful, appears in a bejewelled strapless wedding gown. Her breasts look like cupcakes in a corset.

'Beyoncé,' Ella says. 'Whatever you say about her, an incredible talent.'

'Again, again!' Howard cries, tapping the screen with a dry old finger. The singer reappears, this time in a see-through white teddy, suspenders, and an impossibly tiny G-string, writhing on the bed with a flower in her teeth. Tess feels that the jumbled, reversed order of things – first garter removal, then marriage, then anticipation – is perfect for her father, who is shedding experience, step by step, into a new kind of innocence.

A trolley appears in the doorway, with the tea lady behind it. There had been a tea lady in Howard's chambers, and Tess hopes this one makes his new world seem familiar to him.

'Not for me, thanks,' Ella says, rising and taking Howard's chart from the back of the door.

Then Tess remembers. 'Just a minute!' She fumbles in her handbag and passes the tea lady the Bar Association mug from the pool. The woman fills it from the urn and Tess hands it to her father.

'Thank you, darling,' Howard says. She thinks he might, just, recognise it.

When they are done, she kneels next to him. 'I'll see you in a week, Dad. Remember? I'm going to London.'

'Have a good time in London.' Howard repeats the place name like a fact in a case and she gets a sad knife-flicker in her heart of what it was like when he could keep track, from one day to another, of where she was. He holds her gaze and there is a moment when they don't seem to know whose turn it is to speak. Then he clears his throat and says,

'You were the best thing I never had.'

'What do you mean, Dad?'

When Howard started to lose his mind he had compensated by imbuing the most ordinary statements with sphinx-like gravitas, so that 'indeed' or 'if you say so' could fit any occasion.

'Dad?' She realises she's holding his knee.

'You,' Howard says firmly, 'and your brother.'

He seems to consider the issue settled, but her eyes tear up and she looks at the carer, who is smiling – a kind, closed-mouth, raised-eyebrow kind of smile by which she signals that this is an intimacy she probably shouldn't be witnessing, but then, what can you do?

V

After the children are in bed she finds her passport and finishes packing. Dan is at a work dinner with a delegation of doctors from China. She closes the door to her study and sits on the sofa with the laptop.

Tess has no idea whether, or to what extent, Dan ever explored the warmth and deep sensitivity of the postdoc. To live with someone for a long time requires an element of fiction – the selective use of facts to craft an ongoing story. Also the suspension of disbelief: we must believe a story is real while we are in it, and the same goes, Tess thinks, for a marriage. She used to admire people who described their marriages as open, who told each other about every indiscretion in thought and deed. But what she noticed now was that without editing, or at least a little magical thinking, those relationships had ceased to exist, because their participants simply no longer believed in them.

When she was twenty-one Tess had lived with Mitya. It was for less than a year, but ever since she has kept the memory of him like an Aladdin's lamp inside her, something she can take out from time to time and rub to see it glow. Of course Dan knows about that relationship, but for him it has receded into prehistory. For her, to speak of it now would be to blow out the private flame, small as a pilot light, of another possible life.

She listens to the sounds of the house till it is quiet enough that she feels alone. Then she clicks onto Facebook, finding the white lozenge where she can put in his name to search. Her stomach does a small, strange, long-ago twist.

After she'd finished her arts degree, Tess used her savings from waitressing to go backpacking in Europe, from London to Amsterdam to Paris, then making her way down Italy to Capri, where she got a job as a dog walker. The dogs she cared for were mostly small ones that spent a lot of time in women's handbags and under restaurant tables. She would leash them up, sometimes five or six at a time, like harnessing a team of grateful birds.

She took the same route every day, collecting each dog from its owner's house then taking them along the stone-walled path down the hill. On the cliff side the wall was covered in cascades of astonishing purple bougainvillea; the other, lower side looked out across white houses and terracotta roofs to the bay. She walked through the pedestrian streets of the town, past all the designer shops, the dogs' toenails clicking on the paving. Then she steered her entourage to the quay, where clusters of uniformed hotel porters milled around, waiting for the ferries to spill out their holiday-makers, dazzled and expectant.

In the third week, as she passed a café on the Marina Grande, the white pomeranian started barking at a customer. Tess reddened. As she approached, the man bent to pick something up off the ground.

'*Mi dispiace*,' she said, then in English, 'I'm so sorry. He's never done that before.'

'No,' the man smiled, 'I sorry.' He showed the chicken bone in his hand. 'I asking for trouble.'

She smiled back, a little uncertain, holding onto

the leads. The man pushed his sunglasses onto his head. He was older, maybe close to forty. He wore an open shirt and old leather slip-ons without socks.

'I have terrible English,' he said, stubbing out a cigarette, 'and worse Italian.'

She laughed and he stood up, scattering some coins from his pocket on the table.

'I am walking this way.' He motioned in the direction she'd been going. 'I may accompany you?' By then he was close enough to touch her elbow. 'You are the Lady with the Dogs,' he said as they set off, the first of many things which seemed poetic to her, in that she didn't quite grasp their meaning.

One knock and Charlotte tumbles into the room. It's dark and her mother's face is lit only by the glow of the screen in front of her.

'Do you know where my soccer shorts are?' Charlotte asks cautiously, because sometimes her mother explodes at the expectation that she'll keep in her mind the precise location of everyone's every article of clothing, in its relentless cycle 'from floor to drawer'. But now her mother stares at her as if she hasn't heard the question.

'Mum?'

'Try the washing basket.' Her voice is oddly mild.

'Okay. Thanks.' Charlotte turns to go.

'And put your headgear on,' her mother calls.

'Yessss, Mum.' After Charlotte closes the door she hesitates for a moment, her head tilted. But there's nothing to hear, so she sets off for the laundry.

Tess exhales. She types in his name but doesn't press enter. For one thing, it feels like spying. For another, she is going nose-close to the invisible electric fence of her marriage.

Dmitri (who went by Mitya) was from Moscow, but had been living on Capri for the six years since Russia had opened up, leaving behind a wife and a son not much younger than Tess. Mitya was an artist, making works on canvas out of photographs, collage and paint. They might have been good – they certainly seemed like art compared to the touristy oils of boats and seagulls and the Blue Grotto sold on the quay.

For some days they walked the dogs together. They talked as outsiders talk, bonding over what was foreign and strange to them both in Italy, as if that would make them less foreign and strange to each other. He told her he'd wanted to get far away from the Soviet Union, to a place where its categories did not make sense. Later, she realised that the categories he meant were dissident and nonconformist artist, and underground. But in that moment she was enthralled by the idea itself: that you might escape whatever categories you came from, go somewhere they no longer applied.

Mitya had a favourite beach club, where a restaurant controlled a little stretch of sand. They ate fish at tables with white cloths under a slatted wooden awning, and then sunned themselves on the rocks like seals. They walked the cliff-edges on paved tracks and wandered down to pocket-sized beaches to swim. He was never working and always working – he took photos of her coming out of the water, asleep under a hat. He sketched. He painted late into the night in his studio, by the light of large candles intended for church altars.

After three weeks she moved her things from the hostel to his place, a white-walled house high up behind the town, which he rented from a Neapolitan businessman. The entire second floor was a studio, with a diorama and a darkroom at one end and a futon behind a screen at the other, close to the balcony. The first morning, she found a box of tampons in the bathroom, so that later, even when there was much talk of the two of them being soulmates, she never quite shook the feeling that she was one in a long line of girls.

Tess posed for him in the white diorama wearing only a necklace. It was a cheap but pretty chain with a couple of charms on it that rested below her clavicle; he painted it as heavy, looped links reaching to her navel. In the same way that he could make a flimsy piece of jewellery into a work of art, he did what he wanted with her body. She saw herself repeated across his walls, and understood she had her uses.

Of course it was practically a rite of passage for a girl from the New World to find a European lover for a while – so many of her friends had done it that it seemed almost an organised part of life, like a language exchange. But still, he'd been hers. In Russia he'd hidden paperbacks of Solzhenitsyn and Akhmatova and Orwell in his flat. Now, books lay all about the place in piles. He read everything he could get his hands on, from St Thomas Aquinas to Kundera to Sontag. His parents had survived Stalin's famine and Hitler's war. He talked about the Russian soul, when no boys at home mentioned souls, ever. He was both hopeful and hopeless at once, as if his background had let him in on a secret about human nature she could not yet know. One time he wept openly about failing his son. He didn't want more children.

Tess felt special, plucked from her provincial origins to be the lover of this man, catapulted into the centre of European art (so it seemed to her) by virtue of her youth, her blankness, the fate of having been picked out by him. But she knew at the same time – did all reasonably pretty girls know this? – that she could have been any sentient 21-year-old who walked past the marina café and into his life that day.

And both of them knew she could go home at any moment to another, possible life, which was why he spoke of that option with contempt.

'Well, if you want to go, go.' It was after eight months of living together. Mitya was on the balcony, looking at the water – the ridiculous, bobbing boats – not at her. He didn't say it as though he'd be upset if she left, but as though her leaving would constitute a failure to commit to a more complex life than she might ever otherwise have.

Her hand hovers over the keyboard. She feels the flip in her stomach again. She presses enter.

The site is run by his gallerist in Paris, where it seems he lives now. She scrolls down. His work is much as she remembers it, if perhaps stranger and more washed-out. There are no photos of him. She scrolls so fast the screen blurs.

Finally, there is one picture of him, from two years ago. Older but still recognisable: wide smile, short teeth, square chin. He wears sunglasses and a small-brimmed hat, and has his arms around two young women, also in sunglasses. She can't see enough of him. She scrolls back to the most recent posting, a photo of a grand gallery, in its windows the sign: '*Rétrospective: Dmitri Voronin 1994–2014*'. The opening details are posted: *Vernissage*, 18.30. It is at a gallery in the Marais, in five days' time.

When she wakes next morning Dan is already up and into the breakfast routine – she can hear them in the kitchen. He has let her sleep in.

She zips her case and brings it down. Charlotte is making a green smoothie. The twins are at the bench, their hair still crazy from sleep, but they're in their uniforms. Dan is trying to get broken toast out of the toaster with rubber-tipped tongs. They all look so innocent.

'Anyone seen my computer?' Tess asks over the racket of the blender.

Lorna lifts the white scalloped collar of her school dress and wipes her Vegemite-covered mouth with it.

'That's what that's for!' she cries, delighted to have worked it out. Tom looks down at his shirt, which lacks such a napkin.

'But I don't —'

'Anyone?' Tess cuts him off. Today, Tom's problem is not her problem.

'Gotcha!' Dan says to the toast. Then he gestures to a side table where he's put the computer. 'I charged it for you,' he says.

'Thanks.' She unplugs it, puts it in her carry-on case and sits down to drink her coffee.

Before she calls the cab she goes to find Dan, who is brushing Lorna's teeth.

'They're *so* disorganised at work. I got an email last night asking me to stay for the session on Saturday morning after all. I'm sorry. Will you manage?'

Dan pauses the teeth-brushing.

'Sure,' he says without turning around. 'When does that mean you'll be home?'

'Monday night.'

'No worries,' he says, and he believes her, and does not believe her.

VI

London is more like itself than Tess remembers – like a hologram, or a scene from *Notting Hill*. When she passes a red fire hydrant or phone box (a phone box, still!), or a bobby with a round hat, it all seems exaggeratedly, prettily British. The pubs are decorated with hanging baskets of bright flowers and there's a shop near her hotel that has sold nothing but umbrellas for a hundred and fifty years. She buys Lorna a Princess Kate mask, and Tom a double-decker bus stapler. She hasn't finalised her presentation and is going to have to wing it.

After the conference dinner on Thursday night, she walks around her hotel room, the bathroom, turns on the TV. She should call home but she's too busy having imaginary conversations with Mitya. The scenarios veer from moonlit walks along the Seine followed by passionate lovemaking to gutting humiliation. Perhaps he will be cruel. Or worse, blithe. She feels excited and ridiculous, middle-aged and adolescent, as if she never really grew up.

The next day she excuses herself from lunch and hails a black cab. She climbs into its dark booth, the driver screened off behind glass. The rear-vision mirror frames a pair of neutral, all-seeing eyes. She could tell those eyes anything. But she can't explain what she's doing, even to herself, so she just says, 'Kings Cross St Pancras, please.'

She pays in cash for a ticket on the Eurostar for Saturday and the strangeness of using paper money makes it feel criminal. Back at the conference she can't tell whether the flutter in her stomach is the old one from Mitya, or a new one, from deceit.

On the train to France Tess opens her computer to his Facebook page so she can stare at his hatted, sunglassed face. He seems to have chipped a tooth, though it could be the bad-quality picture.

What does she want from him? The thought of getting her clothes off in front of someone who hasn't had years to acclimatise to her body makes her shudder in the upholstered seat. Though given enough wine and darkness she knows she would, she also knows that this is not about sex. She is looking for something else, some feeling she had then that has been lost.

The room (she pays again with cash) is in a boutique hotel in the 11th arrondissement. It is sweet and clean, with yellow shepherdesses on the wallpaper, but so small there's no space to open her suitcase on the floor and she has to do so on the bed, then close it and stand it upright again when she wants to lie down. It is five o'clock. Tess needs to wait till six-thirty to leave, so as to arrive when plenty of people are already there. She lies down and counts shepherdesses.

Then she gets up, puts on her black dress, and looks at her face in the mirror. Something has gotten hold of her – something ugly and self-pitying, something that wants to take revenge on the unknown, unhappy Sukie, on the entire population of Puerto Rico, on whatever it is that has stolen her father's mind. She dresses it up as 'I deserve this,' as 'You only live once,' and even, as she pushes her hair back off her forehead, 'This is what they do in France.'

In the French taxi she has no urge to confess. They wind through the streets of the 11th, and then

43

the tinier, cobbled ones of the Marais. She does not make eye contact with her reflection.

The car stops. There is no gallery.

'You can't find it?' Tess asks.

'*Mais oui, madame.* We've arrived.'

Tess looks out. The gallery has shrunk from the exaggerated, wide-angle pictures on Facebook to a single shopfront. People are spilling out onto the street, smoking cigarettes.

'Please, keep going,' she says.

'*Compris, madame,*' the driver says.

She gets out two blocks away and walks back, swinging her arms. As she makes her way inside, it occurs to her that Mitya might experience this as an ambush. Too late. Whatever force has taken her over, it can't leave her now. She passes a tall, fat man with a moustache and a fedora surveying the crowd and saying loudly, '*Ou il est, mon p'tit Russe?*' She says, '*Pardon,*' half a dozen times, clinging to a glass of champagne as she turns sideways to slither past the black-clad backs of people talking in hermetically sealed groups. As usual at these things she feels incredibly uncomfortable, and as usual no one is looking at the art, except the sole other friendless person at the end of the room. Her heart beats hard a couple of times, out of rhythm. She scans the room for him, a white room, with ceiling lights in rows shining on his work, which seems, now that she looks at it, to be of weather or moods – pure compositions of colour and form and light. They are not terrible, Tess thinks, but you'd have to bring a lot to them.

About halfway down, she sees him. He is standing with three other people, turned slightly away, but she'd recognise that profile anywhere – flat forehead, straight nose. The fat man in the fedora is closing in behind her. Tess takes a gulp of air and forges on. At times in her life – admittedly more dramatic times, including opening nights, speech-giving, and childbirth – she has had the feeling, as she waited in the wings, or went up to the microphone, or changed breathing strategy, that so much of courage is just being too far in to turn back. A point comes when the cost of retreat seems greater than the dread of annihilation to come. And then a strange, fatalistic quiet kicks in and slows your pulse, giving you strength for the last, calamitous push.

'*Mon pote!*' the fat man cries, right behind her. As Mitya turns he sees Tess without registering her. He raises a hand to his friend, but as he starts to wave, his eyes flick back. And then she sees that his other arm is around – a girl in a black dress. The old feeling floods back: she has been one of so many.

When she reaches Mitya his arms are open.

'It can't be true!' he cries, kissing her four times on the cheeks. 'I thought I saw a phantom!' He's laughing, flushed. His teeth are mottled. He introduces her to the fat man, and to his girlfriend, who kisses her too.

'Ah yes, he's spoken of you,' the girl says. She is curious, not unkind.

Tess forgets their names immediately.

'Are you an artist also?' the fat man asks politely. She shakes her head.

Mitya seems to be moving from foot to foot, or swaying a little, shaking his head too. One side of his collar is above his jacket, the other under.

'*Excusez-nous un petit moment,*' he says, touching his girlfriend lightly on the forearm. 'I show Tess my work.'

The crowd parts for him without trouble and he leads her past a lot of people who, in another life, she might have known. They start at the front, with the most recent work and move back through the last twenty years. The shapes on the canvases gradually change from patterns of bright light in a white sky to a series in which a slate-coloured sea meets the sky at a horizon in the middle of each canvas, and then an earlier period of faceless figures seated alone at tables.

At the far end are the only recognisable humans in the retrospective. Three small photographs of the same girl have been cut out to the shape of her body and pasted into the corner of a painting. She moves closer. It is a cloudscape in shades of pale grey, an imaginary sky out of which Tess's younger, near-naked self seems to have fallen.

'After this,' Mitya lifts one shoulder, 'it all got more . . .' He gestures with his glass to the rest of the room. 'Abstract.'

He uses the word *abstrait*, which can also mean 'hard to understand'. Or, she supposes, both at once.

On their way back to the others he tells her he married a Frenchwoman not long after Tess left Capri. The girl here tonight is his first girlfriend since his wife died fifteen months ago. Before they reach his friends he stops, so she does too.

'When you left,' he says to the floor, 'I felt I survive a plane crash.'

One glass of champagne and her mind is leaping, unfettered. 'But you sent me home.'

'No.' He's looking at her now, as if saying something he has wanted to say for a long time. 'I wanted you to choose. I wanted you not to be in two worlds at once, and only partly in mine.' And then he keeps walking.

She'd thought of herself for so long as having been generic, possibly interchangeable, that the idea that he'd been vulnerable to her comes as a sluice of cold in her veins. She sees she was a heedless, head-hunting child, gathering scalps. On that balcony he was not daring her to choose a life of European complexity over Australian simplicity. He was asking her to make it her real life, by giving up some other, undermining dream.

Then she took home her souvenir of him, her scalp – her lamp – and white-anted her life with it.

Tess gets another drink. She is uncharacteristically chatty with strangers, practising her broken French with no concern for how terrible it sounds. She tells the man in the fedora, 'We were lovers, a long time ago,' and he says, 'I know,' pointing with his glass to the work at the end of the room. Then she tells him, in great detail, about developments in legal publishing.

When she goes to say goodbye, Mitya says, 'I'll see you out.'

On the footpath he leans heavily against the building as he taps a softpack of Gauloises.

'Ridiculous, these non-smoking laws,' he says.

Tess laughs. His hair is entirely silver. He's spilt red wine on his blue shirt.

'*Ça me fait du bien de te voir*,' he says.

'It's good to see you, too.'

He asks about her life and she tells him of Dan, of Charlotte, Lorna and Tom. She almost says, You see: the expected categories, but she doesn't. Because to say that would be the most disloyal thing of all. And because she wants to show Mitya that she has learnt, if only this minute, how to be in the one place.

'*Une grande vie alors*,' he says. 'A big life, then.' He gives a kind of Gallic shrug, lifting his arms out and letting them flop at his sides.

She leans in and kisses him for a long time. It feels anatomical.

She has to get home.

VII

After landing, Tess turns her phone on as soon as the overhead announcement says they may. A message from Dan on the screen: *Everything is fine but we're all at your Dad's. Come straight here?*

At reception a wrinkly, suntanned woman she hasn't seen before, wearing half-glasses with a tortoise-shell-coloured plastic chain attached to them, tells her Howard has been 'upgraded'. Tess raises her eyebrows.

'He wandered on down to the pub on the corner,' the woman says.

'That's all right, isn't it?'

'It was eleven o'clock in the morning.'

'Was it shut?' Tess feels defensive about her father in general, and about wandering in particular. She's so tired she can still feel the movement of the plane.

'Nah, but he asked the publican to call him a taxi. To take him back to his *house*.'

Wanting to go home is a crime here, apparently. But Tess can't bear to think about the possibility of Howard seeing the For Sale sign out the front of the place, like a plaque on a memorial site. The woman seems to be waiting for something, maybe her punchline.

'Driver was a local bloke,' she smiles. 'Brought him back. I'm new, but it happens a bit, I'm told.'

Tess sees that she's not cruel, she's just not yet skilled in delivering delicate news to relatives, the tricky two-step of comfort and truth. The woman directs her to Howard's new, more secure room.

From the end of the long carpeted corridor she hears the singing, a vaguely familiar tune. When she reaches the doorway there they all are, with Ella – even Charlotte, in a red 1950s bandana and full makeup – singing and swaying to the music from the iPad on Howard's lap. The twins rush up from the floor and grab her around the hips. The others smile but keep belting out the song, something poppy about a girl knowing someone wants her back. Tom turns his head up.

'It's Beyoncé, Mum,' he says.

Ella conducts with her hands from the chair next to Howard, who in this motley, raucous company looks as sane as anyone. Dan and Charlotte are standing behind him. Dan catches her eye.

When they get to the start of the chorus Ella moves her hands wildly and everyone sings louder, finishing with a rousing cry. Someone, it seems, has been the best thing the girl never had.

Tess snorts and starts laughing, shaking her head. She lets go of Tom and Lorna to pinch her nose.

'That bad?' Charlotte watches her mother warily.

'No, we're good!' Lorna cries. 'We are!'

Tess can't stop laughing or she'll cry. What a fool she was to think her father meant those words for her. It feels like trickery, like sleight-of-heart.

'What is it, Mum?' Charlotte's voice is worried now, or annoyed, or both. Ella and Dan watch.

'No – you're great.' Tess wipes her eyes. 'You're all really great. It's just . . . I thought . . .' She fumbles in her bag for a tissue. 'I thought *someone*,' she flicks her eyes to Howard, who is busy tapping the screen again, 'said those words to *me* the other day.'

Even though her mother keeps sort of laughing, Charlotte can see that her eyes are full. That's when she understands that people go on forever wanting things from their parents that they don't have to give.

'I'll leave you guys to it, then,' Ella says. As she passes Tess in the doorway the younger woman pauses. She's quite large, and they are nearly touching. 'You know,' she says quietly, 'sometimes you might just need someone else's words. That's what a song's for, right?' Ella turns her head back to the old man. 'See you tomorrow, Howard.'

Howard keeps smiling at the spot where Ella was. Tess looks at his fine, vacant face. He clears his throat. 'How was Paris?'

'The conference was in London, Dad,' she says gently.

'Come on, Mum,' Charlotte scoffs.

Something isn't right.

'What about your side trip?' Charlotte is taking her phone out of her pocket. 'To gay Par-ee.' Charlotte holds up the phone and taps the Life360 icon. The screen turns into a map with five quick pins, impaling all of them at this spot on the planet – one!-two!-three!-four!-five! – right here in Hopetown Village.

'Bring anything back for us?' Charlotte is asking.

'Yay, presents! Presents!' The twins jump up and down.

Tess looks at Dan, whose face is unreadable.

'Wait till we get home,' she says.

On the way out of the hospital the twins run down the long curving ramp for the disabled, and Charlotte dashes to catch them before they reach the drive-in entrance. Dan walks slightly ahead of Tess. Her eyes fix on the whorls of dark hair on his crown.

'Bring me any art?' he says to the space next to him, where she isn't. 'I saw his gallery opening on your computer.'

She catches up. 'Why didn't you say anything?'

'Say what? I'm not your keeper.'

The kids are gathered at the carpark pay machine, the twins checking for lost change in the slot.

'Is that all you're going to say?' she asks.

Dan stops, to stay out of earshot. There are bruise-coloured half-circles under his eyes. He doesn't deal in a world where things can be changed by editing, or thinking of them differently. He deals in facts, events, symptoms. He puts one hand to the back of his neck.

'I knew where you were.' He speaks slowly, not angry but in a tight voice. 'And I think I know why.'

'Why?' She's hardly entitled to be asking the questions, but his eyes hold hers.

'You were looking for something.' He says it gently, like an admission.

In the car the twins fall asleep, their necks crooked on the booster seats. Even Charlotte dozes off. Tess has never seen anything as beautiful as her sleeping children. She watches the white lines on the road flicking past. She thinks of Chekhov's 'The Lady with the Dog', those famous closing lines. Of course she can only remember the start of them: 'And it seemed as though in a little while the solution would be found, and then a new and splendid life would begin . . .' And then there was something about there being a long, long road before them, and that the most complicated and difficult part of it was only just beginning.

But that isn't it. It is something from the middle of that story that best suits where she is, in the middle of her life. It's hard to remember exactly, but as she looks at Dan – his spray of acne scars, his sweat-stained shirt – her heart contracts and she understands that this is her one and only life.

After Howard was buried under a plaque with his name and dates on it ('At least you know where he is,' Tom said, by way of both comfort and truth) she thought often about what she took to be his last words before, as Charlotte put it, he 'started speaking only in Beyoncé'. James had dozed off in the chair by the window. Howard gripped Tess's hand to raise himself off the pillow and said, 'It was so much better than I'd thought.'

They were his own words and she couldn't get her mind around them. Their combination of celebration and regret seemed to her the greatest gift he could have given.

ACKNOWLEDGEMENTS

With grateful acknowledgment of Miley Cyrus's song 'Wrecking Ball', and Beyoncé's 'Best Thing I Never Had'. And many thanks to Georgina Wilson, a brilliant reader and Russian specialist. Warmest thanks too to Paspaley Pearls, from whom the inspiration, time and resources came for this story.

PENGUIN
SPECIALS

OTHER PENGUIN SPECIALS YOU COULD TRY:

Also by ANNA FUNDER

All That I Am

*WINNER OF THE 2012 MILES FRANKLIN
LITERARY AWARD
Winner of the Barbara Jefferis Award,
the Independent Bookseller's Award for Best
Debut Fiction, the Indie Book of the Year 2012,
the Australian Book Industry Award Best Literary
Fiction, the Australian Book Industry Award
Book of the Year 2012, the Nielsen BookData
Bookseller's Choice Award 2012.*

When Hitler comes to power in 1933, a tight-knit group
of friends and lovers become hunted outlaws overnight.
United in their resistance to the madness and tyranny
of Nazism, they flee the country. Dora, passionate and
fearless; her lover, the great playwright Ernst Toller; her
younger cousin Ruth and Ruth's husband Hans find refuge
in London. Here they take awe-inspiring risks in order to
continue their work in secret. But England is not the safe-
haven they think it is, and a single, chilling act of betrayal
will tear them apart.

Some seventy years later, Ruth is living out her days in
Sydney, making an uneasy peace with the ghosts of her
past, and a part of history that has all but been forgotten.